TM

SUPER-PETS!

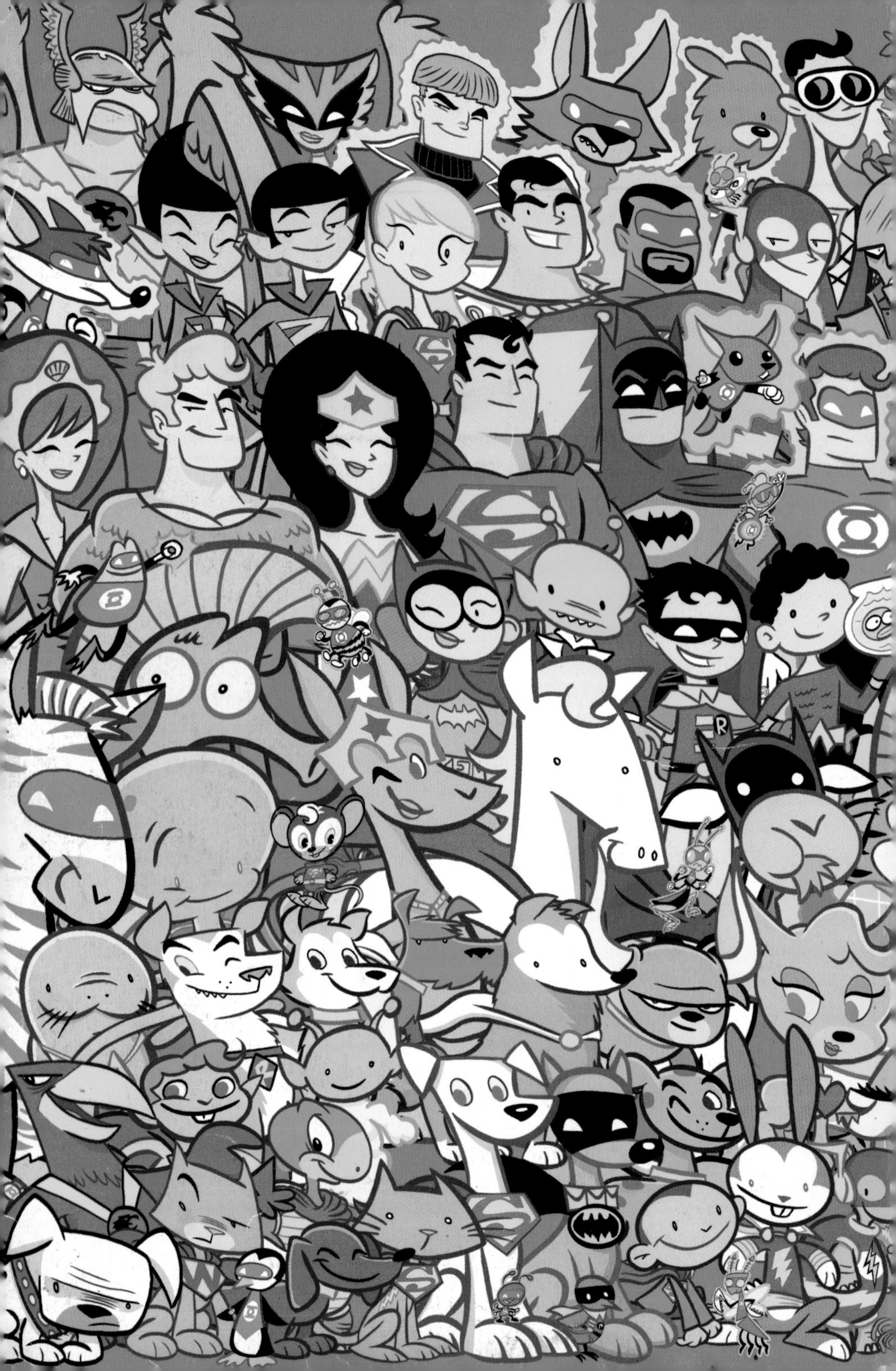

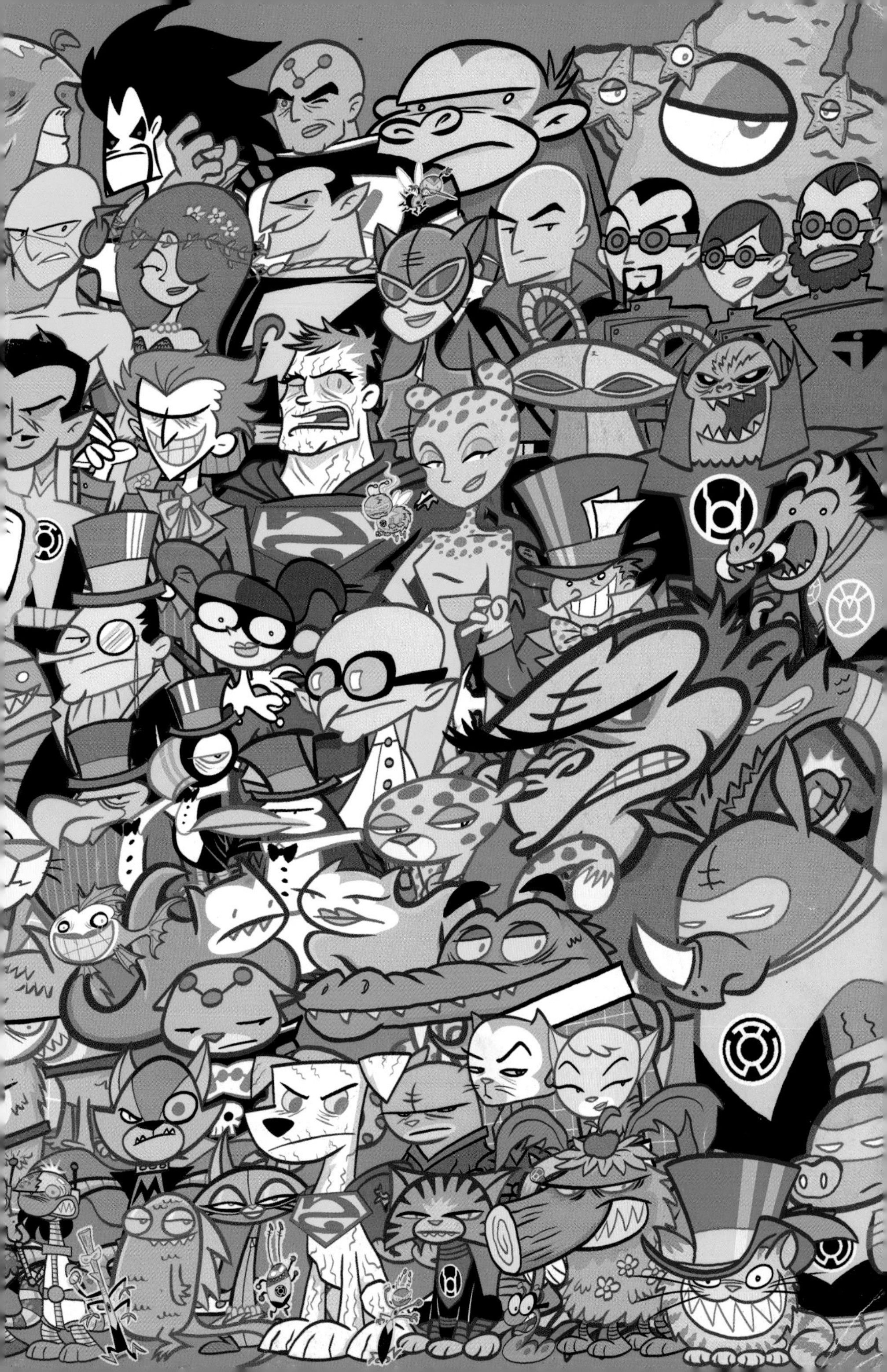

DC™

SUPER-PETS!

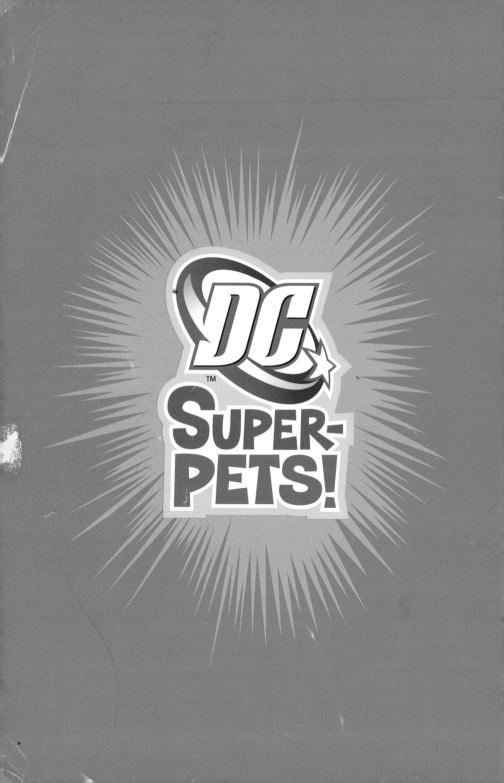

by Sarah Hines
Stephens

SUPER-PETS
SHOWDOWN

illustrated by
Art Baltazar

Superman created by
Jerry Siegel and Joe Shuster

Picture Window Books™
a capstone imprint

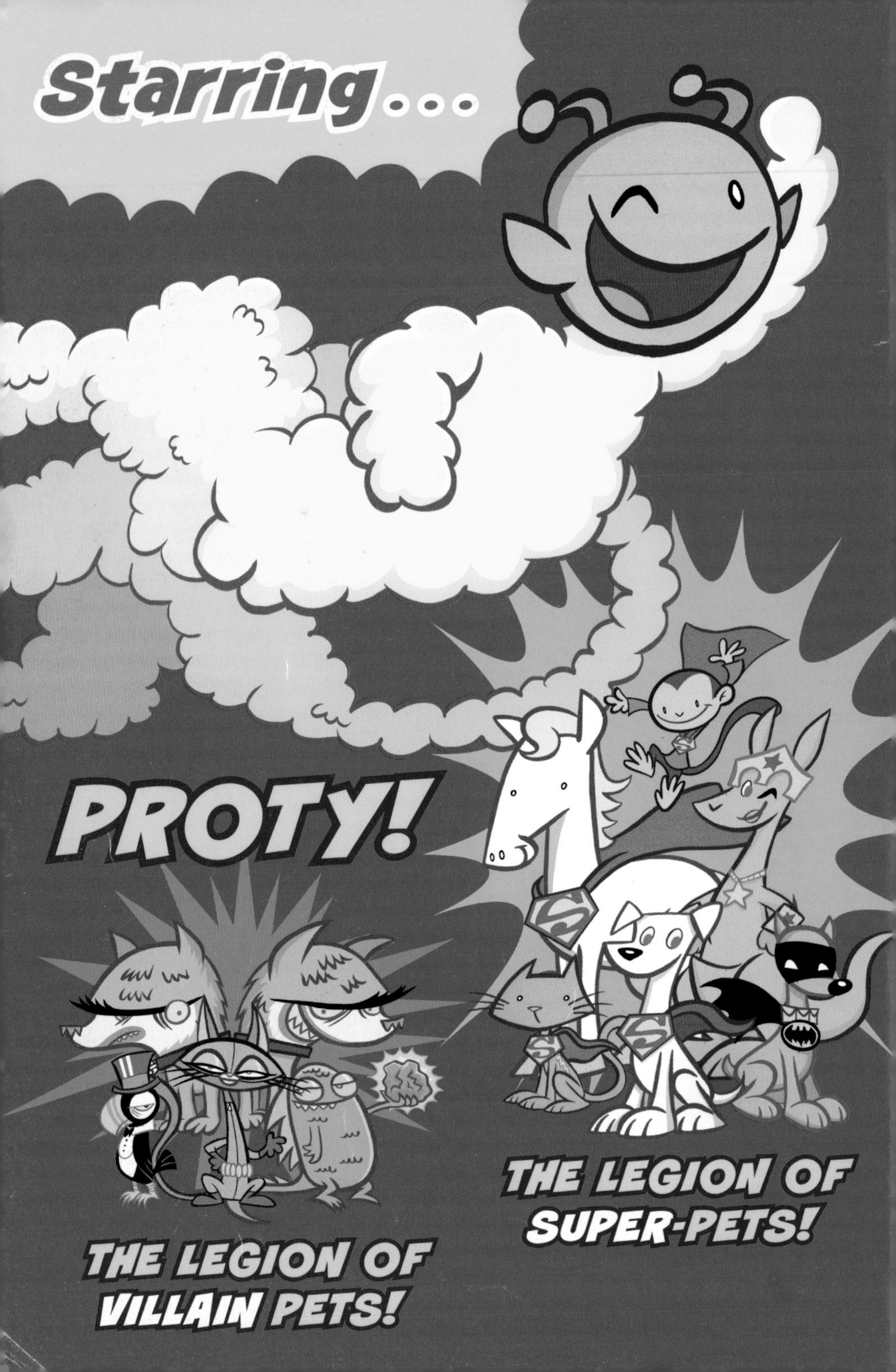
Starring...
PROTY!
THE LEGION OF SUPER-PETS!
THE LEGION OF VILLAIN PETS!

TABLE OF CONTENTS!

SUPER-PET HERO FILE 015:
PROTY

Mind-reader

Shape-shifter

Super Hero Owner:
CHAMELEON BOY

Race: Llorn

Place of Birth: Antares system

Age: Unknown

Favorite Food: Marshmallows

Bio: After traveling to a planet in the Antares system, Chameleon Boy adopted Proty as his protoplasmic pet.

Super-Pet Enemy File 000:
THE LEGION OF VILLAIN PETS

IGNATIUS **ARTIE PUFFIN** **ROZZ** **CRACKERS** **GIGGLES**

LEX LUTHOR **THE PENGUIN** **CATWOMAN** **THE JOKER** **HARLEY QUINN**

Super-villain Owner File 000:
THE LEGION OF DOOM

5

PET SITTING

Inside the **Hall of Justice, Streaky**
curled into a ball on Supergirl's chair.
He and his friends were keeping an eye
on the **Justice League** headquarters.

"*Meow*! Wake me if anything goes
wrong," the Super-Cat told the other
Super-Pets with a yawn.

The World's Greatest Heroes

didn't often leave the Hall of Justice

in the paws of pets. But they had been

called to a meeting aboard their secret

satellite. However, the animals they

left in charge were not just any pets.

They were the **Legion of Super-Pets!**
And today, the headquarters was their
own **Kennel of Justice!**

Batman, Superman, and the other
heroes had only been gone a few hours.
So far, everything was quiet — quiet
enough for a catnap, in fact.

"Go ahead and snooze,"
Krypto barked at the sleepy cat. "I can
handle anything that goes wrong. I
have all of the powers of **Superman!"**
The Super-Dog aimed his freeze breath
at a plate of Kanga's kibble.

FWOOSH! In an instant, he had turned it frosty white. The Dog of Steel was thrilled to be left in charge.

Jumpa, Wonder Woman's amazing Kanga, was not so thrilled with her frozen meal. She snorted at Krypto.

"You're not the only Super-Pet in the Legion," Kanga reminded him. "I'm as fast as **Wonder Woman!**"

 To show her skills, Jumpa ran four laps around the Kennel of Justice in no time.

"That's nothing," **Comet** whinnied.

"You should see how high I can fly!"

The Super-Horse prepared to fly out of

one of the headquarters' windows.

At that moment, **Proty,** the smallest

of the Legion of Super-Pets, spoke up.

"We all have superpowers," Proty reminded the other pets. "There's no need to show off."

"Well, I don't know if I'd call your powers *super*, Proty," Krypto joked with his friend.

PLOOP! Proty slumped down. He looked like a puddle with antennae sticking out. His feelings were hurt. *It's true,* he thought. *I'm just a glob of goo.*

Proty didn't have flashy powers like the other pets. He wasn't super-fast or super-strong. He couldn't melt or freeze objects. Sure, Proty could change into other things and read thoughts, but he didn't find those powers very exciting.

Wishing he could hide, Proty made himself look like a plate of food on the table. He tried not to read what the other pets were thinking, but he couldn't help it.

Proty sensed that they all felt a little sorry for him. None of them believed he would be of any real use if they ever came upon danger.

 **"Don't worry about it, Proty,"** said Ace the Bat-Hound. But Batman's Dog Detective didn't have a chance to cheer up his blobby buddy.

Suddenly, an alarm sounded in the Kennel of Justice. **It was coming from the Justice League's computer!** The pets gathered around the screen. This was a real emergency. With the super heroes in space, the pets needed to take care of it themselves.

Images flashed on the screen, along with a plea for help. Poachers were capturing kangaroos and wallabies in Australia by the hundreds. The animals were in danger.

Instantly, Jumpa leaped to the

rescue! Almost as soon as Jumpa had

gone, the alarm sounded again.

Another call for help was coming in.

This time, a giant storm off the coast of Maryland was threatening to sweep herds of wild ponies out to sea. With a whinny and toss of his white mane, Comet the Super-Horse took flight to save them. **WHOOSH!**

Then, another alarm rang out.

This call sounded as bad as the others. Hurricane floodwaters had stranded thousands of pets on the roofs of buildings. If someone didn't fetch them to safety, they could starve.

All over the globe, animals were in trouble. Krypto, Ace, Streaky, and the others didn't wait to help the pets in peril. They prepared to fly off at once.

"You're in charge, Proty," Krypto said before he disappeared.

With their capes and tails flying behind them, the furry heroes were off.

And Proty was all alone.

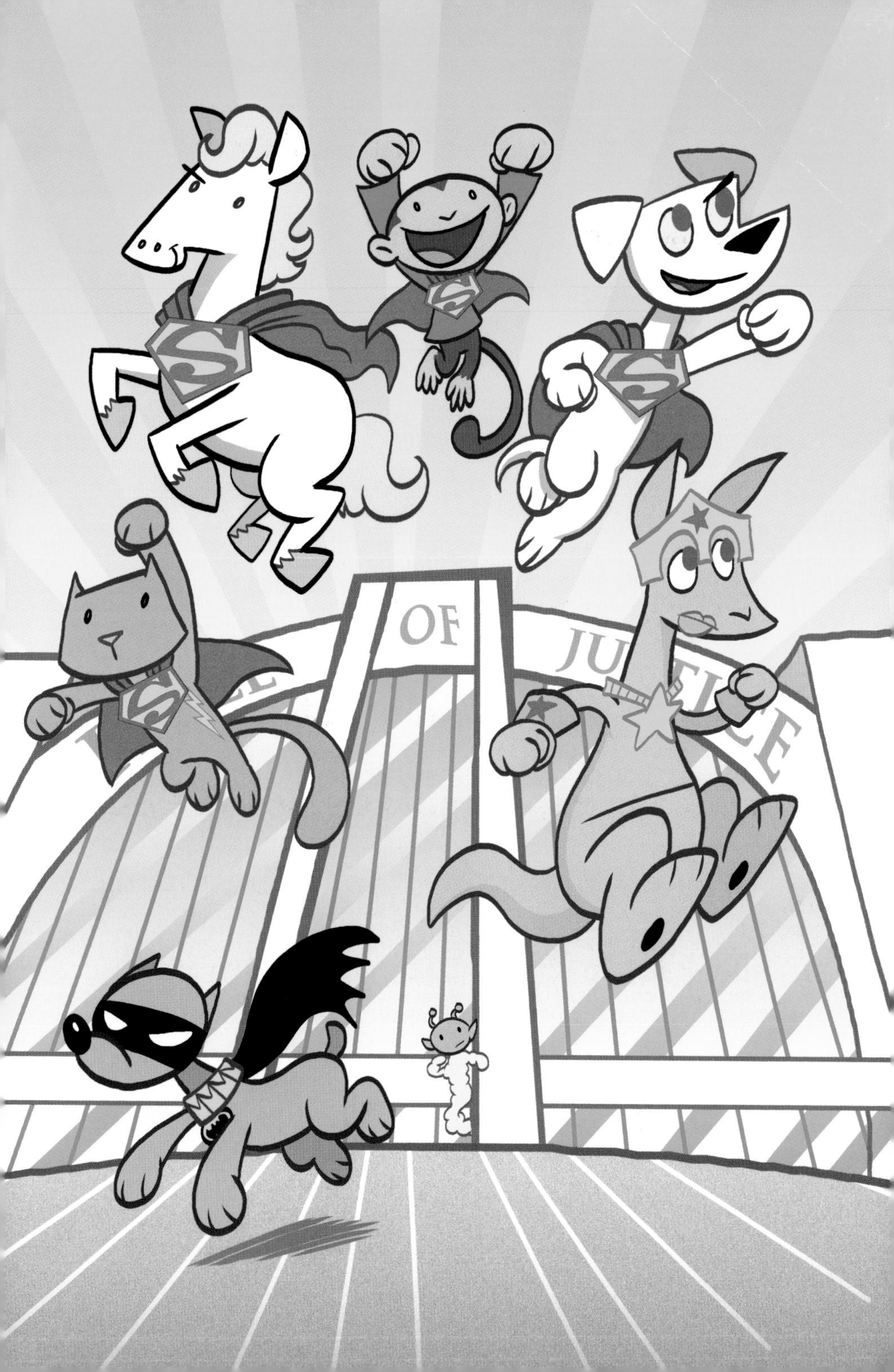
OF

Chapter 2

GLOB OF GOO

Proty let out a heavy sigh.

He was finally in charge, but now he had nothing to do! He wanted to help the others. However, since he couldn't fly, his only responsibility was sitting by the computer . . . and waiting.

With everyone gone, the Kennel
of Justice was surprisingly quiet. No
pets were showing off. Alarms weren't
ringing. All was well . . .

Or was it?

Proty's powers were few, but he could
sense things. And suddenly, Proty felt
that something wasn't quite right.

The gooey do-gooder melted into
another puddle on the floor. A bad
feeling rippled across his surface.

Proty wondered if the rest of the pets had been right. He was not very super.

Maybe, Proty thought, *all I am is a spineless super zero.*

Just then, Proty started to shiver again. The shape-shifting Super-Pet was picking up on something evil. In fact, he was picking up on more than one troubling tingle. He was sensing a whole herd of havoc.

WHAM-O!

Suddenly, the doors of the Kennel of Justice blew open.

To avoid being seen, Proty quickly
changed into the shape of a chair.
Then he spotted them. **"The Legion
of Villain Pets!"** Proty said to himself.
The evil animals had come to take
over Justice League headquarters.

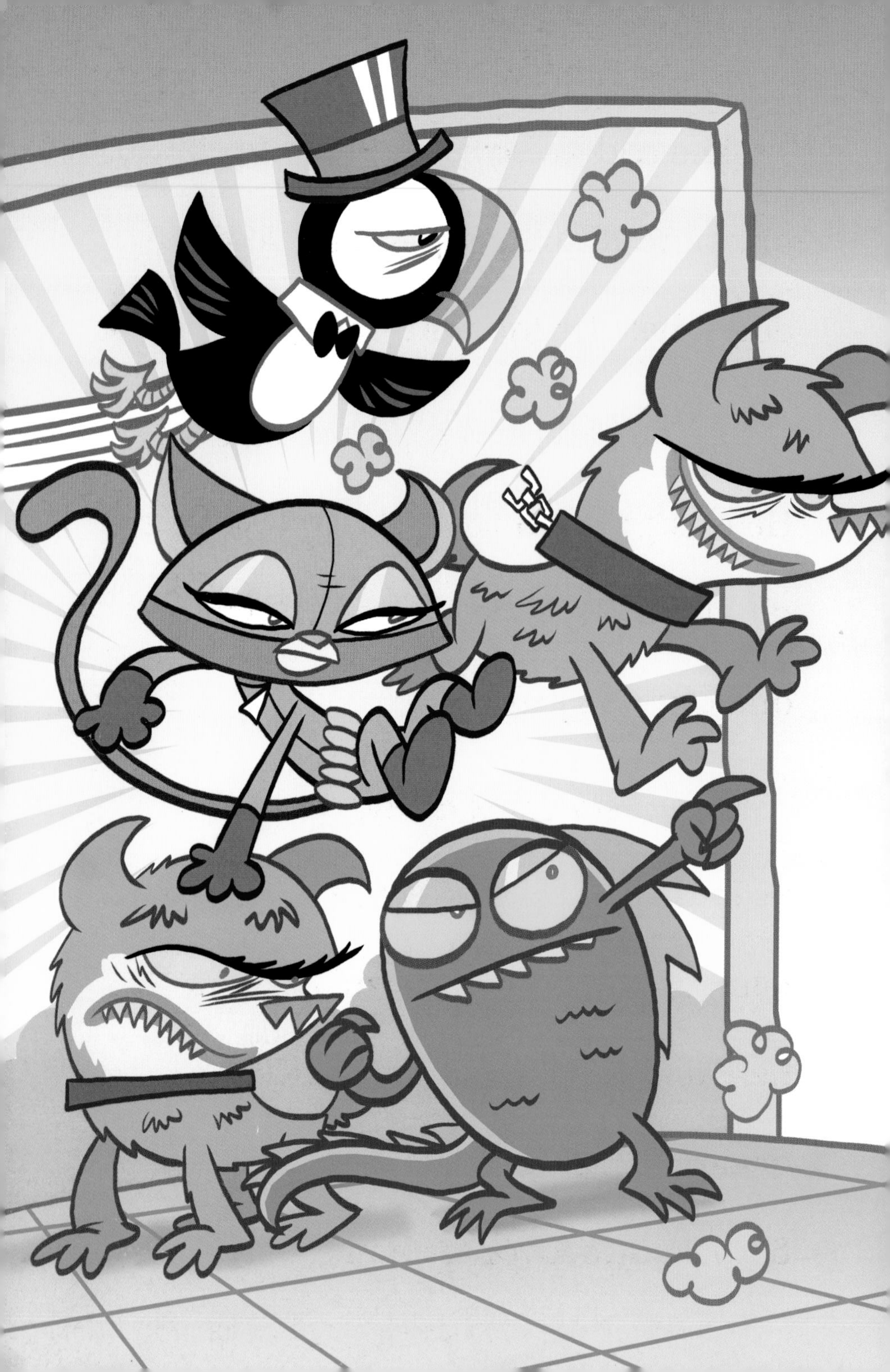

"The cat's away!" Ignatius Iguana

announced, strutting inside. "And the

dogs, too!" He laughed loudly.

Ignatius was Lex Luthor's sidekick.

He was greedy and mean. But most of

all, he simply hated Streaky, Krypto,

and anything super.

"Not every cat is away," purred

Rozz, the evil Catwoman's favorite

feline. "After all, I'm a cat, and I'm

here and ready to play." With a

graceful leap, she landed on Ace the

Bat-Hound's favorite chair.

Rozz revealed her razor-sharp claws.

Then she slashed wildly at Ace's chair.

How she would love to sink her claws

into the Bat-Hound himself.

"Gulp!" Proty looked on with fear.

As more villain pets entered, Proty stayed quiet. He spotted the **Joker's** hyenas, **Giggles** and **Crackers,** snickering in the corner. **Artie,** the **Penguin's** puffin and the brains behind the **Bad News Birds** was there, too.

 **"Getting rid of those silly Super-Pets was a piece of cake,"** Ignatius said.

"Meow!" purred Rozz. "Those flying flea-bags took to the skies the second they got those phony phone calls!"

 "Ha! Prank calls are hilarious," Giggles giggled.

"And easy," cackled Crackers.

"Maybe too easy," added Artie the Puffin. He snapped his beak nervously.

Ignatius scratched his scales. "The bird brain is right," he said. "Spread out and make sure we're alone."

"Hahaha! We don't take orders!" Joker's hyenas exclaimed.

"Quiet, you two!" shouted Rozz. **"You're not in charge here."**

Nearby, Proty could read the evil cat's thoughts. Rozz didn't like being bossed around either.

Without another word, the villain

pets spread out in all directions. They

checked every corner of the Hall.

Only Artie stayed behind. **He had a**

bird-brained plan of his own!

When the others were gone, the evil Puffin moved toward the Trouble Alert computer. He sat down . . . right on top of poor Proty!

"**Ow!!**" the squishy Super-Pet let out a slight squeak.

Luckily, Artie was too busy to notice his slimy seat. **He snickered through his colorful beak and punched the high-tech computer buttons.**

Proty focused on the bird's thoughts. He needed to find out the puffin's plan.

Using his mind powers, Proty quickly got the scoop. His protoplasm ran cold. The villain pets were not just taking over the hero headquarters. They were planning to bring down the entire Justice League! And Artie wanted all of the credit.

The villain pets were going to use the Justice League's own technology against them. And so far, everything was going according to their plan.

First, they had herded the heroes to a single target — the satellite. Now, they planned to pull the satellite out of orbit and send it crashing into Earth!

Proty couldn't let that happen. The spineless Super-Pet might not be as super as some, but he had been left in charge. **He was going to do his duty!**

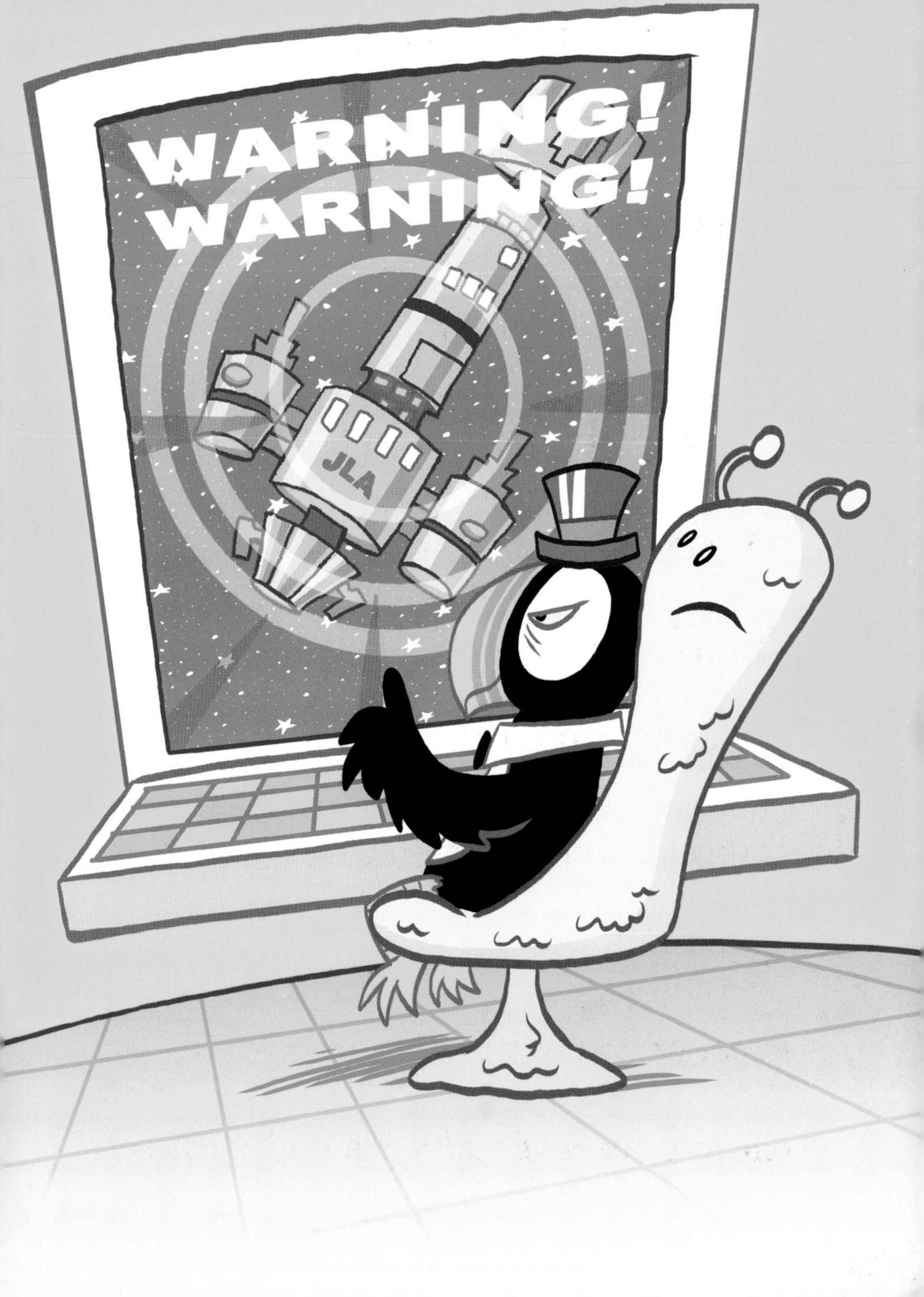
WARNING!
WARNING!
JLA

Chapter 3

FACE OFF!

Artie the Puffin finished setting the computer. Then he stood and placed his flipper over a big red button. It would pull the Justice League Satellite out of orbit and send it toward Earth.

"Bye-bye!" shouted the bad birdie.

Without a moment to lose, Proty

changed into a copy of Catwoman's

evil Siamese. **"Hold on there, Puffy!"**

the fake cat hissed.

Artie spun. **"Rozz!"** he shouted with

surprise. "Where did you come from?"

 **"Never mind that,"** replied the copied cat. "I'm here now, and I'm in charge of pushing the button."

Artie's feathers ruffled. "Who says?" squawked the puffin. "I want to do it!"

"Neither of you are pushing that button," Ignatius said, walking in and flexing his spines. "I'm the boss!"

"Ha! No way!" Giggles barked. The hyenas were back as well.

"Yeah, there are two of us! So we're in charge," Crackers added.

"Never! You're a pack of clowns!" Artie snapped.

While the Villain Pets argued, Proty snuck over to the high-tech computer. He sent a message to the Super-Pets and reprogrammed the computer.

"Hey! Get away from there, Prissy Paws! I'm in control here," Ignatius cried. He had spotted the cat at the computer, and he didn't like it.

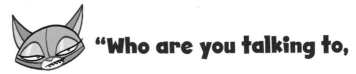 **"Who are you talking to, lizard lips?"** the real Rozz asked. The furious feline had returned and was standing in the doorway.

"Huh?" Ignatius stared at Rozz, confused. Then he spun and looked at the computer seat across the room. In the spot where he had seen Rozz, there was nothing but a puffin feather.

"Maybe we should all just chill out," said Artie. The evil bird pulled a pair of ice dice from under his wing. The dangerous weapons clattered on his flipper. If the dice hit the floor, they would freeze whoever was closest.

"Haha! Artie's right," added Giggles. "We could all use a good laugh."

"Knock knock," Crackers said, following his partner's lead.

 "Who's there?" Artie replied.

 "The end of," Giggles said.

"The end of who?" asked the puffin, shaking his dice faster.

"The end of you," the hyenas said together. They weren't laughing now. They were snarling, drooling, and ready to attack!

 **FWOOOOOSH!**

 **RUFF! RUFF!** The wild animals

leaped just as Artie threw the dice. The

mangy beasts froze in midair and fell

to the ground like blocks of ice.

 **CRAAACKLE!**

"Yow!" Rozz jumped to a higher perch. Things were getting ugly!

Ignatius saw his chance. The lizard lunged for the big red button. He wanted to take down the Justice League all by himself.

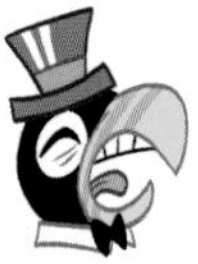 **"Leaping lizards!"** shouted Artie, spotting Ignatius. He quickly rolled his ice dice again. **CRAACKLE!**

The evil iguana froze like a Popsicle.

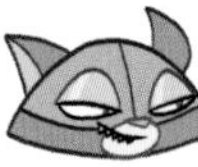 **"Just you and me now,"** Rozz purred.

"Not quite," a voice interrupted.

Rozz and Artie spun toward the

entrance of the room. In the doorway

stood each member of the Legion

of Super-Pets! Well, not exactly. The

whole herd of heroes was really just

Proty in disguise!

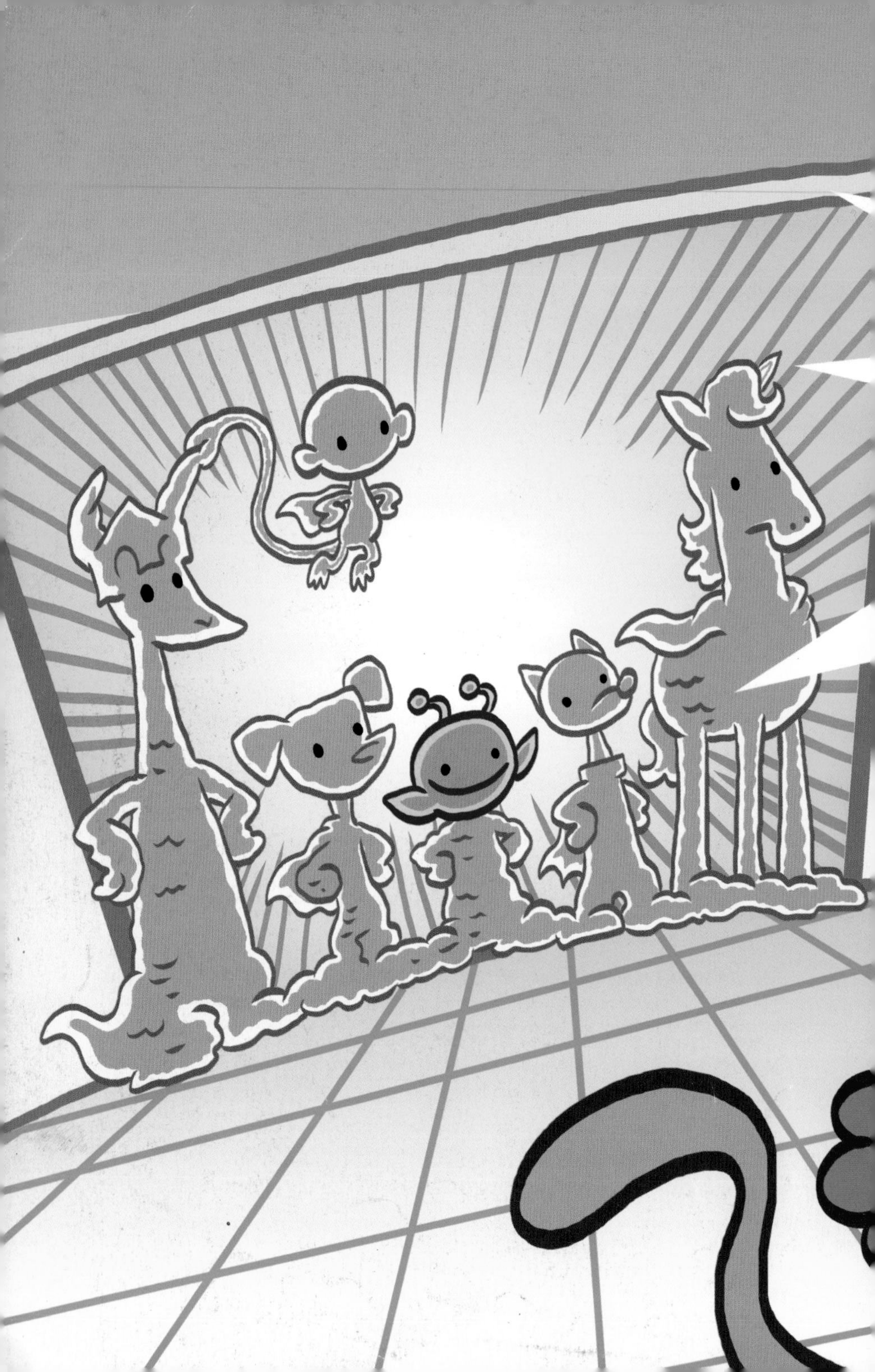

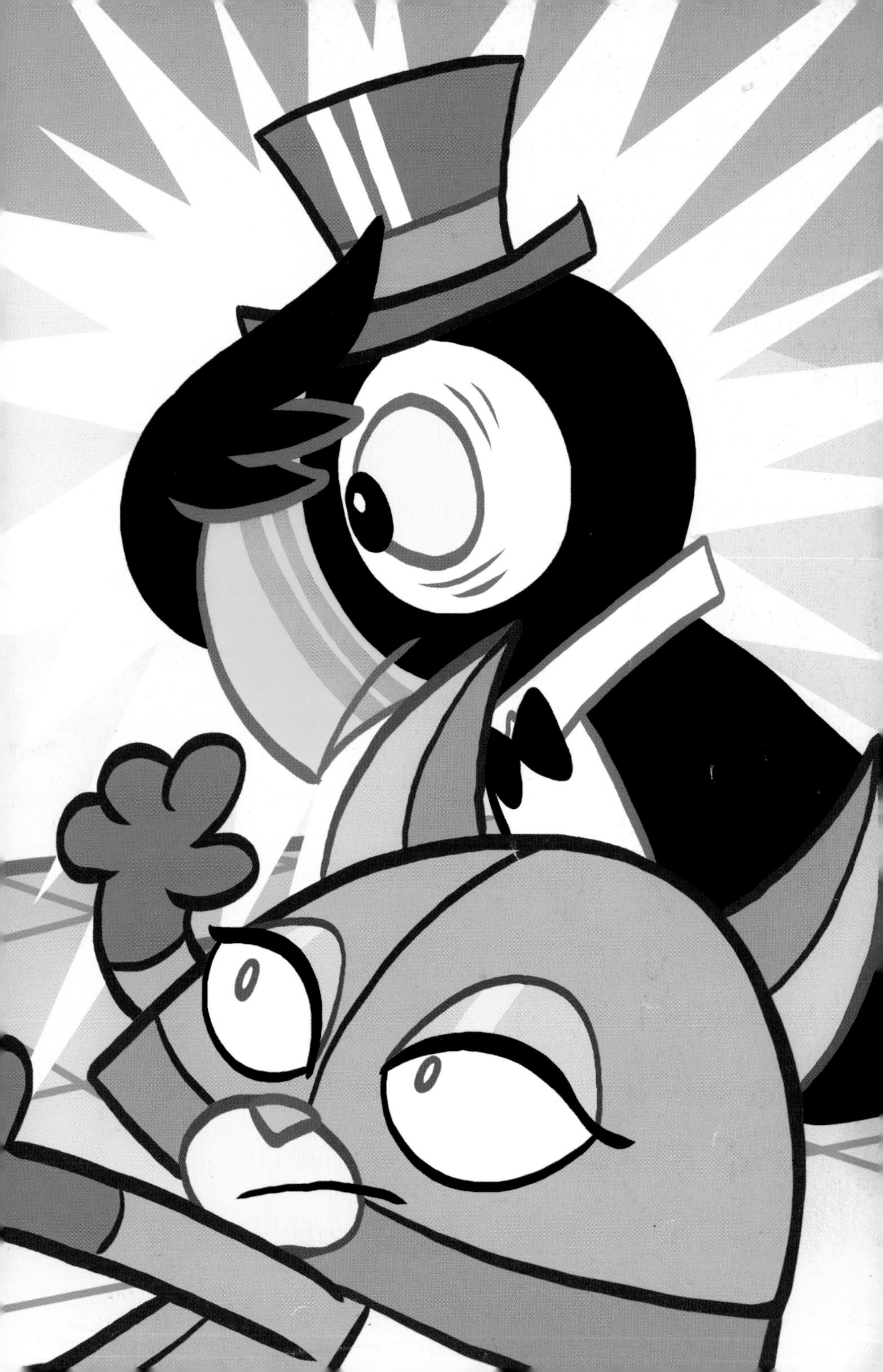

 **"I thought we took care of**

them," shouted Artie. The cold-hearted

bird started shaking with fear.

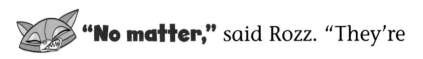 **"No matter,"** said Rozz. "They're

too late to save the Justice League!"

The evil feline leaped into the air. She

landed on the computer and hit the big

red button with her paw. *CLICK.*

WHAM! Instead of taking down

the satellite, the entrance to the room

slammed shut. Proty's plan had worked.

At that moment, Crackers, Giggles, and Ignatius started to unfreeze. The troublemakers were ready for a fight.

"Well, well," said Rozz. "Looks like the perfect match-up. I hope you're ready for a Super-Pet Showdown!"

"**Wrong again!**" said the Super-Pets together. "**It's time for a lockdown!**"

Suddenly, the Super-Pets merged back into **one, powerful Proty.** The spineless hero smiled. Then he changed into liquid and flowed under the door of the sealed room.

A short time later, Krypto, Ace, and Streaky arrived back at the Hall. When they saw the gang of pets Proty had captured, they could hardly believe their eyes. Jumpa and Comet were impressed, too.

 **"Good job, Proty,"** Krypto said.

"Looks like you're pretty super after all," Streaky admitted.

"Speed and power aren't everything," Jumpa agreed.

Comet nodded.

Proty smiled. The gooey do-gooder could read in his friends' thoughts, and on their faces, that they were all proud of him. **He felt pretty proud of himself, too.**

KNOW YOUR HERO PETS!

1. Krypto
2. Streaky
3. Beppo
4. Comet
5. Super-Turtle
6. Fuzzy
7. Ace
8. Robin Robin
9. Batcow
10. Jumpa
11. Whatzit
12. Hoppy
13. Storm
14. Topo
15. Ark
16. Fluffy
17. Proty
18. Gleek
19. Big Ted
20. Dawg
21. Paw Pooch
22. Bull Dog
23. Chameleon Collie
24. Hot Dog
25. Tail Terrier
26. Tusky Husky
27. Mammoth Mutt
28. Rex the Wonder Dog
29. B'dg
30. Sen-Tag
31. Fendor
32. Stripezoid
33. Zallion
34. Ribitz
35. Bzzd
36. Gratch
37. Buzzoo
38. Fossfur
39. Zhoomp
40. Eeny

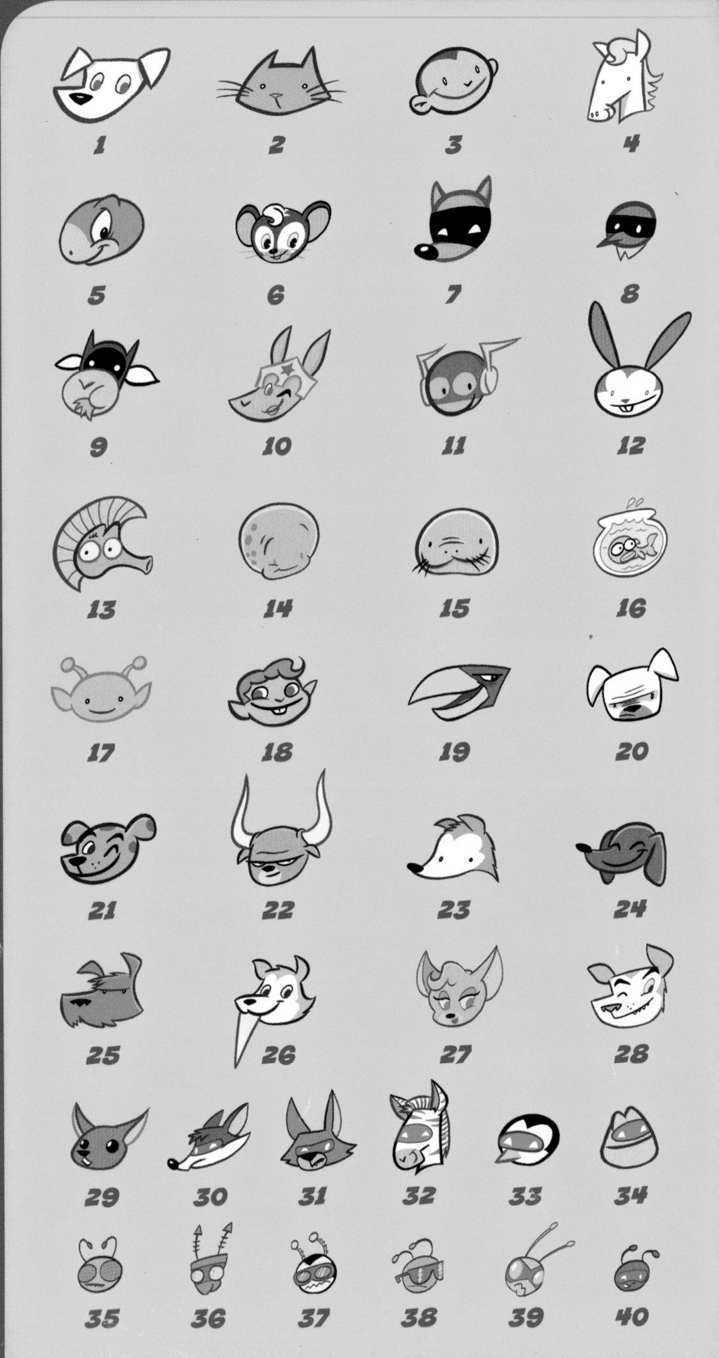
1
2
3
4
5
6
7
8
9
10
11
12
13
14
15
16
17
18
19
20
21
22
23
24
25
26
27
28
29
30
31
32
33
34
35
36
37
38
39
40

KNOW YOUR VILLAIN PETS!

1. Bizarro Krypto
2. Ignatius
3. Brainicat
4. Mechanikat
5. Crackers
6. Giggles
7. Joker Fish
8. Rozz
9. Artie Puffin
10. Griff
11. Waddles
12. Mad Catter
13. Dogwood
14. Chauncey
15. Misty
16. Sneezers
17. General Manx
18. Nizz
19. Fer-El
20. Titano
21. Mr. Mind
22. Sobek
23. Bit-Bit
24. X-43
25. Starro
26. Dex-Starr
27. Glomulus
28. Rhinoldo
29. Whoosh
30. Pronto
31. Snorrt
32. Rolf
33. Squealer
34. Kajunn
35. Tootz
36. Eezix
37. Donald
38. Waxxee
39. Fimble
40. Webbik

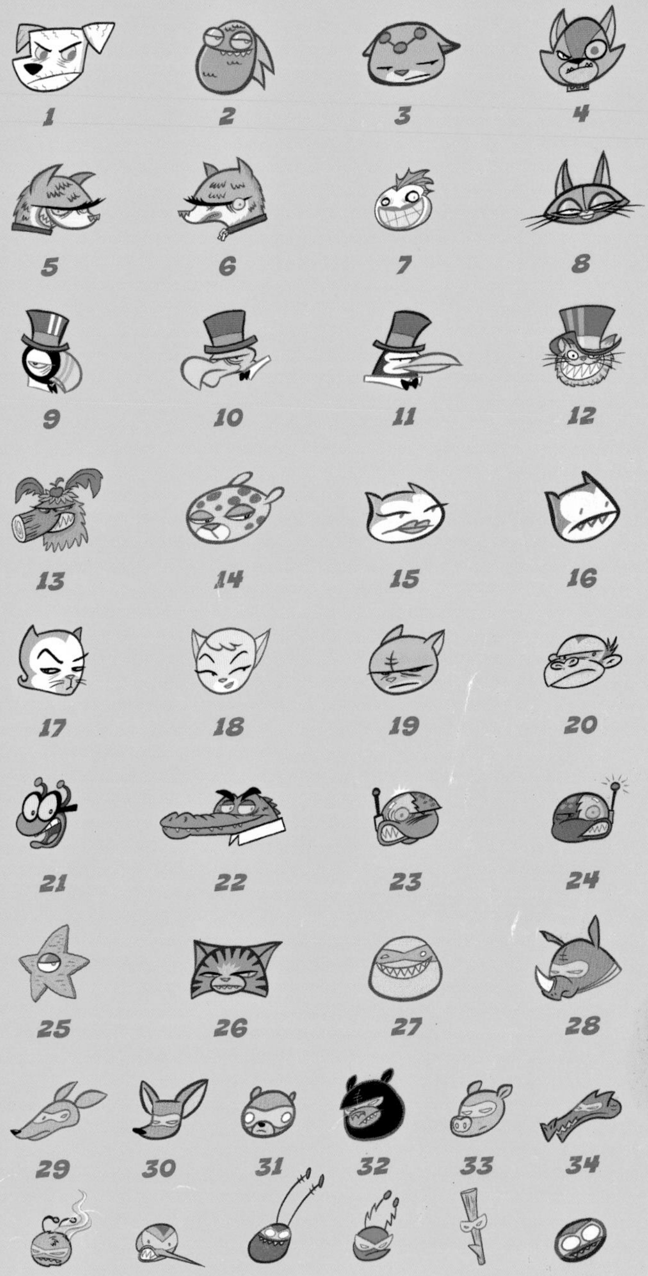
1
2
3
4
5
6
7
8
9
10
11
12
13
14
15
16
17
18
19
20
21
22
23
24
25
26
27
28
29
30
31
32
33
34
35
36
37
38
39
40

MEET THE AUTHOR!

Sarah Hines Stephens

Sarah Hines Stephens has authored more than 60 books for children and written about all kinds of characters, from Jedi to princesses. When she is not writing, gardening, or saving the world by teaching about recycling, Sarah enjoys spending time with her heroic husband, two kids, and super friends.

MEET THE ILLUSTRATOR!

Eisner Award-winner Art Baltazar

Art Baltazar is a cartoonist machine from the heart of Chicago! He defines cartoons and comics not only as an art style, but as a way of life. Currently, Art is the creative force behind *The New York Times* best-selling, Eisner Award-winning, DC Comics series Tiny Titans, and the co-writer for *Billy Batson and the Magic of SHAZAM!* Art is living the dream! He draws comics and never has to leave the house. He lives with his lovely wife, Rose, big boy Sonny, little boy Gordon, and little girl Audrey. Right on!

WORD POWER!

antenna (an-TEN-uh)—a feeler on the head of an insect (or alien)

duty (DOO-tee)—something a person must do

headquarters (HED-kwor-turz)—the place from which an organization or group is run

justice (JUHSS-tiss)—fair behavior or treatment

kennel (KEN-uhl)—a shelter where dogs, cats, and other animals are kept

poachers (POH-churz)—people who catch fish or animals illegally on someone else's land

prank (PRANK)—a playful or sly trick

responsibility (ri-spon-suh-BIL-uh-tee)—a duty or job

satellite (SAT-uh-lite)—a spacecraft that is sent into orbit around Earth

ART BALTAZAR SAYS:

HERO DOGS
GALORE!

SPACE CANINE
PATROL AGENCY!

KRYPTO THE
SUPER-DOG!

BATCOW!

FLUFFY AND THE
AQUA-PETS!

PLASTIC
FROG!

JUMPA
THE KANGA!

STORM AND THE
AQUA-PETS!

STREAKY
THE SUPER-CAT!

THE TERRIFIC
WHATZIT!

SUPER-TURTLE!

BIG TED
AND DAWG!

Read all of these totally awesome stories today, starring all of your favorite DC SUPER-PETS!

GREEN LANTERN BUG CORPS!

SPOT!

ROBIN ROBIN AND ACE TEAM-UP!

SPACE CANINE PATROL AGENCY!

HOPPY!

BEPPO THE SUPER-MONKEY!

ACE THE BAT-HOUND!

KRYPTO AND ACE TEAM-UP!

B'DG, THE GREEN LANTERN!

THE LEGION OF SUPER-PETS!

COMET THE SUPER-HORSE!

DOWN HOME CRITTER GANG!

THE FUN DOESN'T STOP HERE!

Discover more:

- Videos & Contests!
- Games & Puzzles!
- Heroes & Villains!
- Authors & Illustrators!

@ www.capstonekids.com

Find cool websites and more books like this one at www.facthound.com Just type in Book I.D. 9781404864863 and you're ready to go!

Picture Window Books™

Published in 2013
A Capstone Imprint
1710 Roe Crest Drive
North Mankato, MN 56003
www.capstonepub.com

Copyright © 2013 DC Comics.
All related characters and elements are trademarks
of and © DC Comics.
(s13)

STAR25288

Cataloging-in-Publication Data is available
at the Library of Congress website.
ISBN: 978-1-4048-6486-3 (library binding)
ISBN: 978-1-4048-7216-5 (paperback)

Summary: While the Legion of Super-Pets
protects the universe, their headquarters
are attacked by the Legion of Villain Pets!
Thankfully, Proty, the shape-shifting Super-
Pet, is still aboard the doomed den. Will this
spineless specimen finally prove he's more
than just a pile of goo?

Art Director & Designer: Bob Lentz
Editor: Donald Lemke
Creative Director: Heather Kindseth
Editorial Director: Michael Dahl

Printed and bound in the USA.
009919R

DC™

SUPER-PETS!

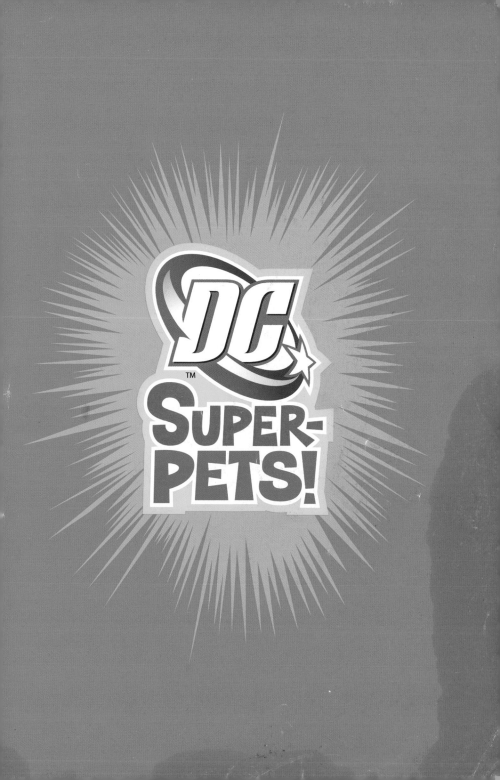

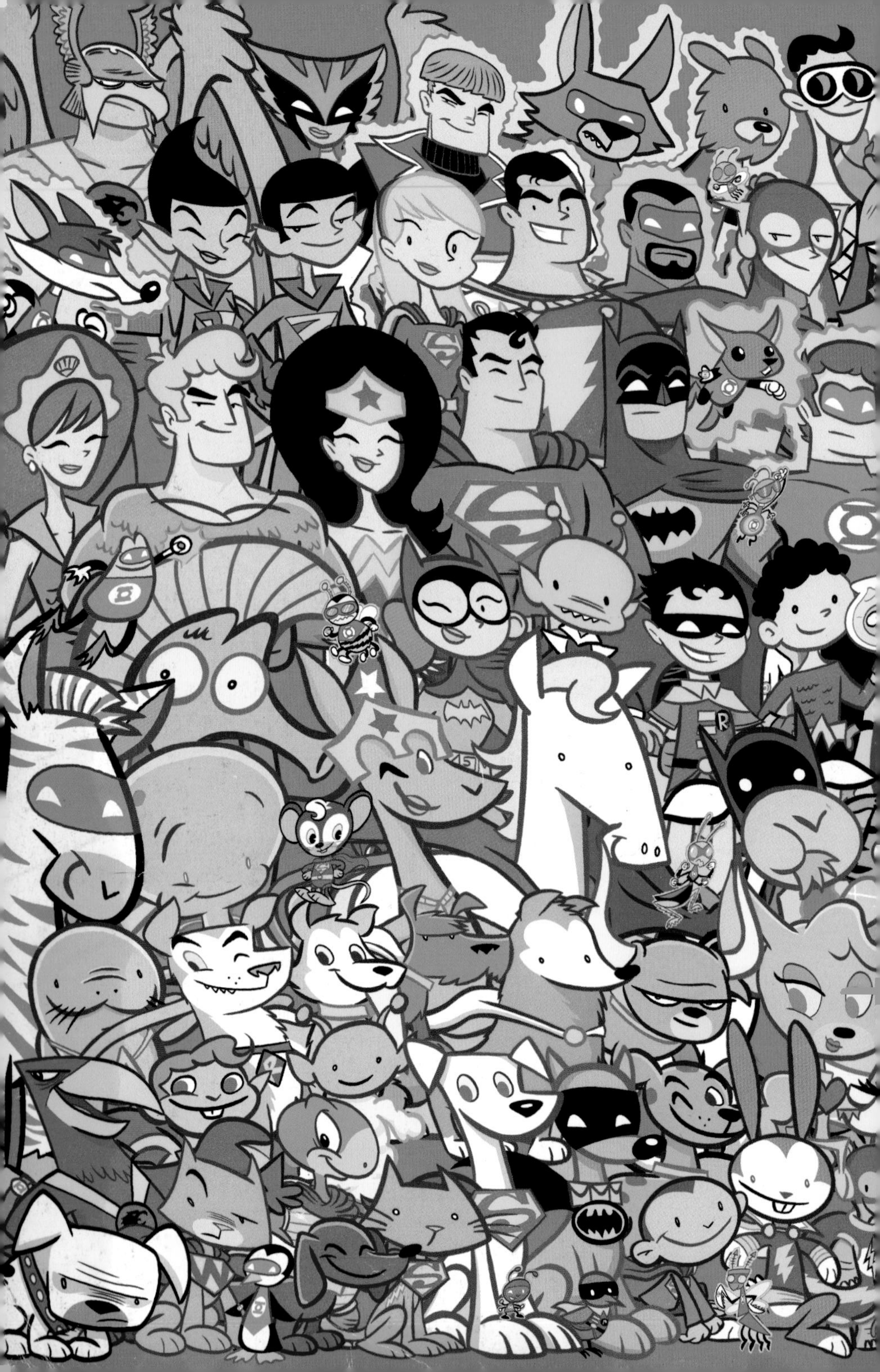

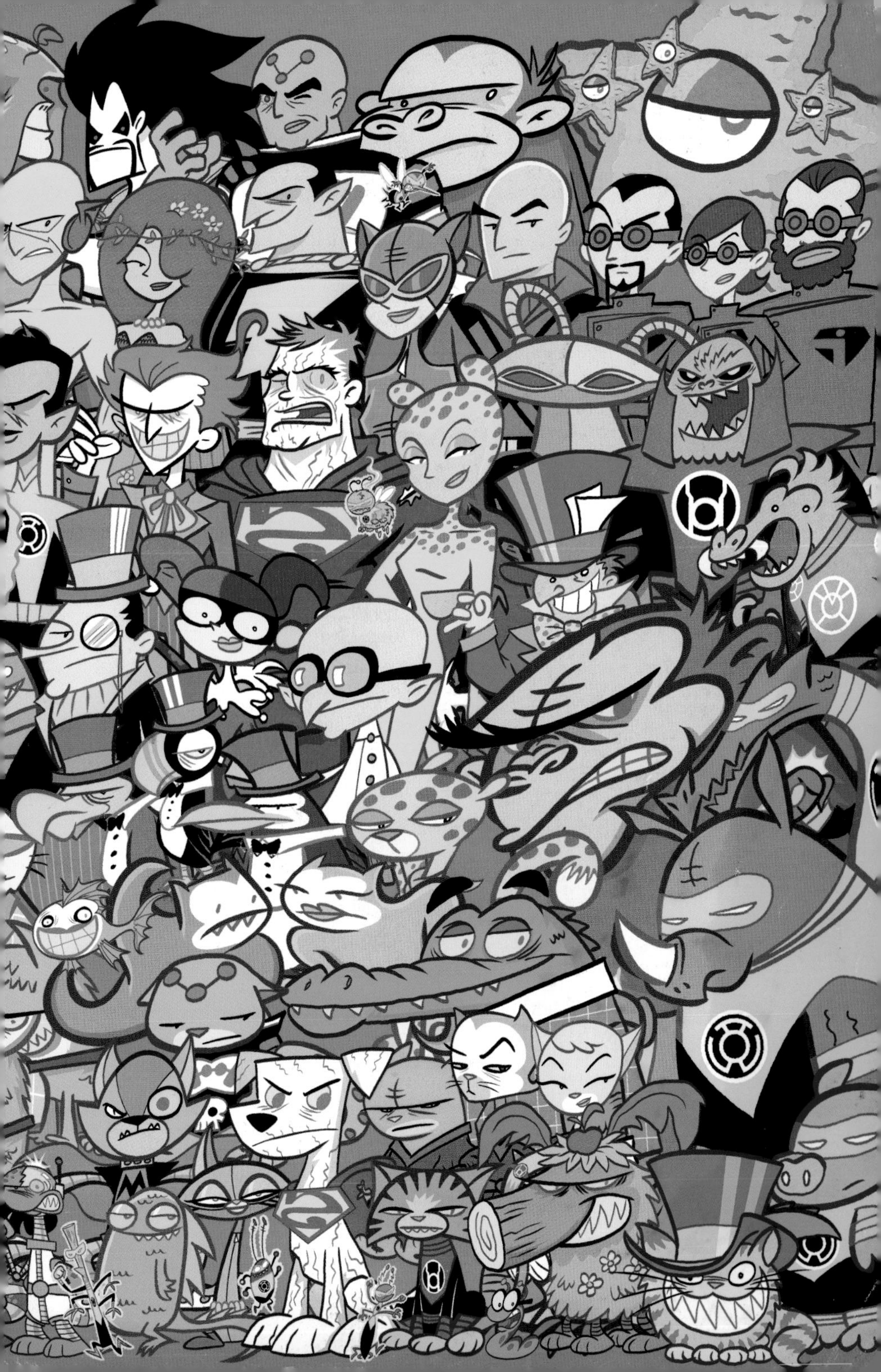

DC™
SUPER-PETS!

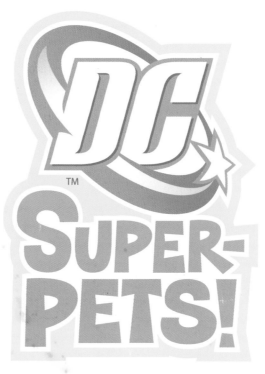